Piper the Puppy
VISITS THE DOCTOR

pat a cake

Sweet Shop

Health Centre

Pharmacy

Café

Piper's House

Glossary

Mummy

Piper

Daddy

Finn

Hoggle

medicine

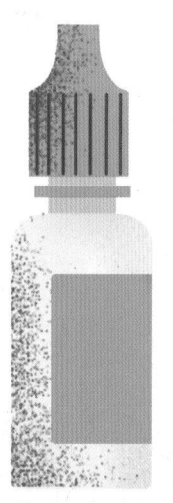

first aid box

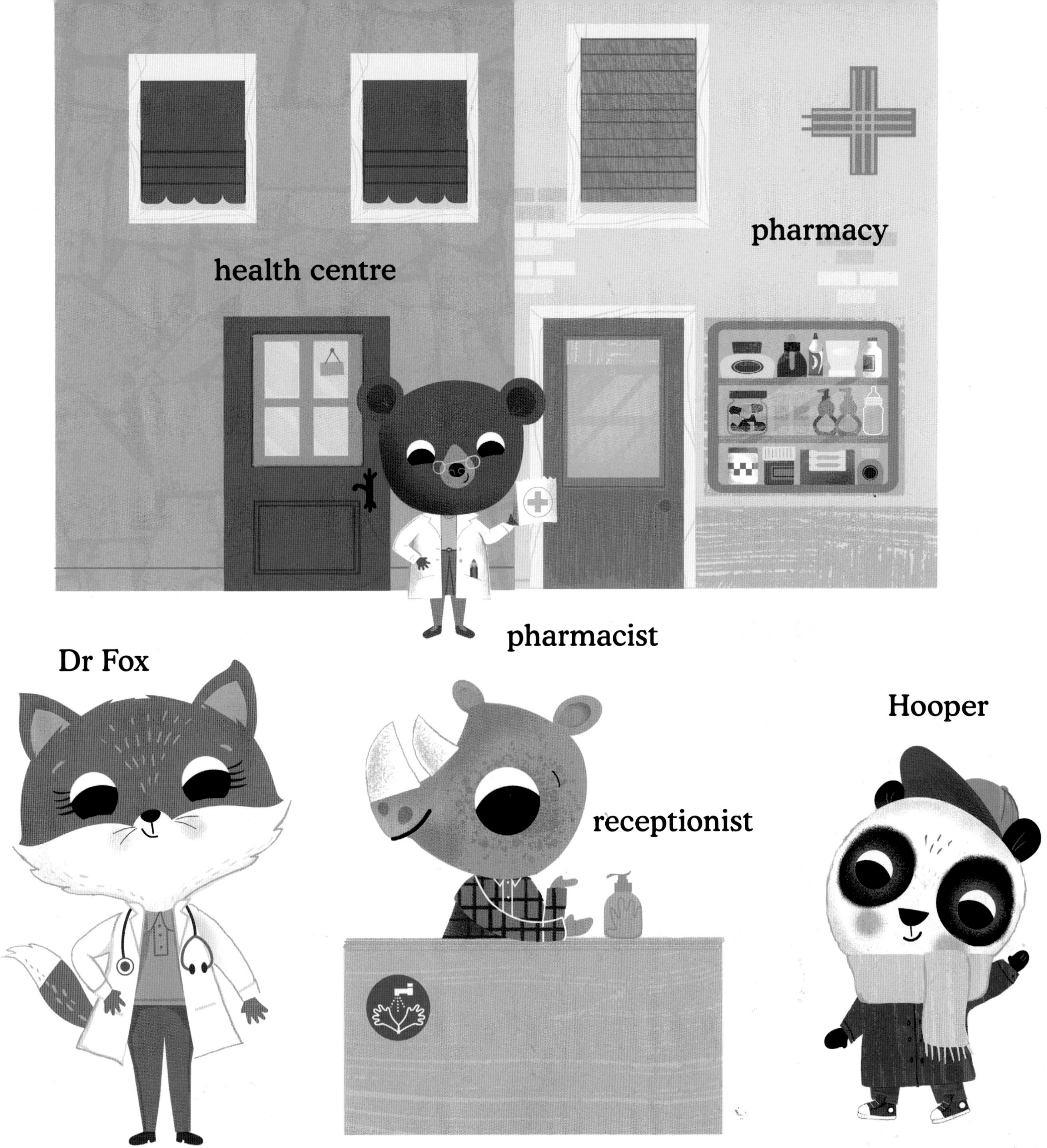

health centre

pharmacy

pharmacist

Dr Fox

receptionist

Hooper

When Piper wakes up one morning, her ear is really sore.
She strokes it gently. "Ouch! That hurts!" she cries.

Piper is poorly. Her head
is hot and she feels shaky.

Piper goes into the kitchen, where Mummy is making breakfast.

"Would you like some eggs, Piper?" Mummy asks.

"I'm not hungry," says Piper.

"What's wrong?"
Mummy asks.
"My ear hurts and I
don't feel very well,"
says Piper sadly.

Daddy gets the first-aid
box. He finds a white
thing with a little button
on the side.

"What's that?" asks Piper.
"It's a thermometer," says Finn. "It measures how hot your body is."
Daddy puts the thermometer gently into Piper's mouth. It makes a
little beep.

"You need to go to the
doctor," says Finn.

"Doctor Fox is very nice," says Mummy. "She will make you feel better."

Mummy takes Finn to school while Piper and Hoggle get into the car with Daddy. Piper hugs Hoggle very tightly.

"Here we are at the Health Centre," says Daddy.

"Hello," says the receptionist behind the counter.
"Hello," says Daddy. "Piper is here to see Doctor Fox."
The receptionist smiles. "Take a seat in the waiting room."

Daddy sits down and Piper snuggles up next to him.

Just then, Hooper arrives with Mrs Panda.

"What's wrong with you, Piper?" asks Hooper.

"I've got a poorly ear!" explains Piper.

"I've got a sore throat," whispers Hooper. His voice is very croaky.

Dr. Fox

"Piper?" says the receptionist. "Doctor Fox is ready to see you now."

Piper tucks Hoggle under her arm and follows Daddy into Doctor Fox's room.

"Hello," says Doctor Fox. "How can I help you today?"
Piper hugs Hoggle tightly. She tries to speak but her voice
comes out as a tiny squeak.

"My ear hurts,"
she whispers.

"Oh dear!" says Doctor Fox. "Would it be OK if I have a little look?"
Piper nods.

"I'm going to shine this special torch inside your ear. It might tickle a little bit," explains Doctor Fox.

"Hmm!" says Doctor Fox. "Your ear is a little bit red on the inside."
"Oh!" says Piper.

"I think you've got an ear infection," remarks Doctor Fox.

Piper is scared. She starts to cry. Daddy gives her a cuddle.

"Don't worry," says Doctor Fox. "I can give you some medicine to make your ear as good as new."

"I don't like medicine," says Piper, sniffing.
"It tastes funny."

PRESCRIPTION

"Ah!" says Doctor Fox.
"You don't have to taste
this medicine. It goes in
your poorly ear."

Doctor Fox writes something on a
piece of paper and gives it to Daddy.

Outside the Health Centre, Daddy takes Piper into a shop.

"Why are we going in here?" asks Piper.

"This is the pharmacy," says Daddy. "This is where we get your medicine."

"Would you and your teddy like a sticker?"
"He's a hedgehog!" says Piper.
Doctor Fox laughs. "Silly me!"

Daddy gives the piece of
paper from Doctor Fox
to the pharmacist.

After a few minutes,
the pharmacist calls out,
"Medicine for Piper!"

"Let's go home," says Daddy.

Mummy lays a cosy blanket on the sofa.
"Lie down here, Piper," she says.

Daddy puts
two drops
of medicine
in Piper's
poorly ear.

Piper closes her eyes and cuddles Hippety, Hoggle and Bear.

When she wakes up, Daddy brings her some dinner on a tray.
"How's your poorly ear?" says Finn.
"Still sore," says Piper, sadly.

Mummy takes her off to bed.

When Mummy wakes Piper up the next morning, she touches her ear very gently. She turns her head from side to side, just to be sure.

"What are you doing, Piper?" asks Mummy.
"I'm seeing if it hurts," says Piper.

Mummy sits on the edge of Piper's bed. "Does it hurt?"
Piper gives Mummy a big hug. "No!" she says. "I feel MUCH better!"

"Great news!" Mummy says. "Let's go and make breakfast for everyone."
"Yes, please!" says Piper. "I'm HUNGRY!"

Storytime Scramble

Here are some pictures from the story. Point to them in order they happened and try to retell the story.

Sweet
Shop

Health Centre   Pharmacy

Café

Piper's House

Train
Station

Grocery Shop

Fire
Station

POLICE
STATION

School